RISSY NO KISSIES

Katey Howes
illustrated by Jess Engle

Carolrhoda Books
Minneapolis

"Oh, the nestlings are just darling,"
cooed Miss Bluebird over tea.

"I can see that they like tickles,
they like treats, and they like me!

"Now I wonder if this little one
would kiss me on the cheek."

"NO KISSIES!"

Rissy chirruped with a most emphatic squeak.

"How surprising!" squawked Miss Bluebird.
Then she laughed as if amused.

"We know lovebirds all love kisses—
I think Rissy is confused."

Rissy's mama kissed her brothers
as she tucked them in the nest.

Rissy's sister kissed her stuffy
as she snuggled down to rest.

Rissy's daddy smoothed her feathers,
and he puckered up his beak.

"NO KISSIES!"

Rissy chirruped with a most emphatic squeak.

"Has she caught a germ?" Dad wondered,
very worried for his chick.

"We know lovebirds all love kisses—
I think Rissy's getting sick."

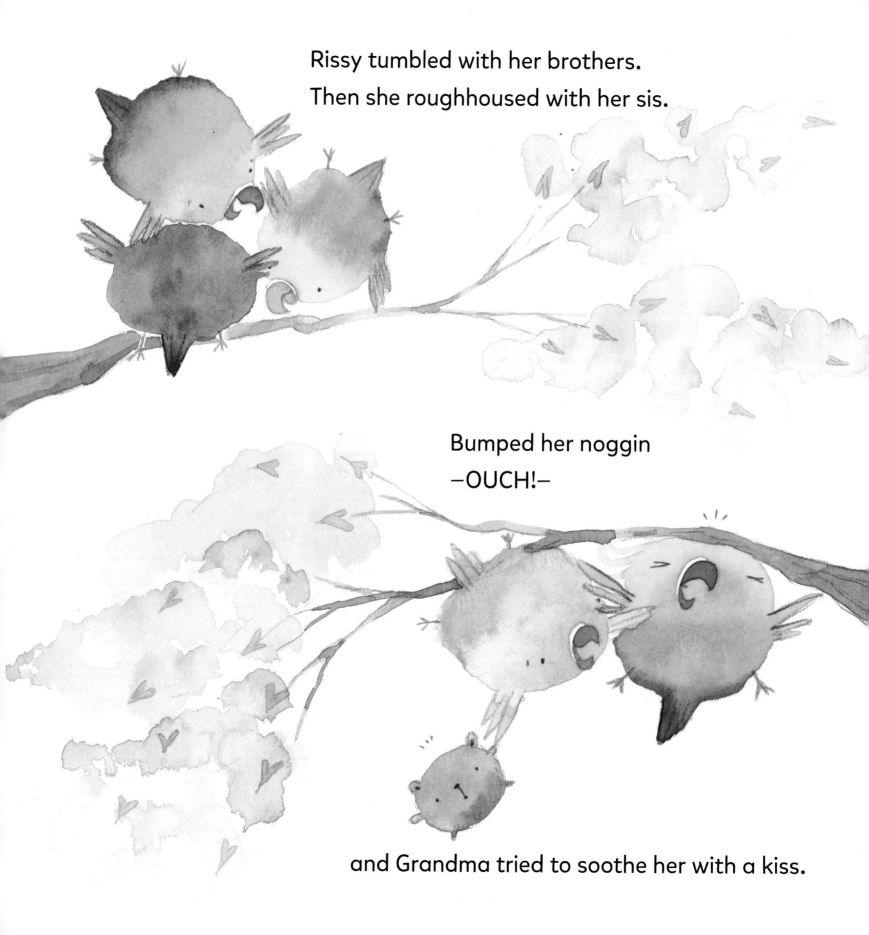

Rissy tumbled with her brothers.
Then she roughhoused with her sis.

Bumped her noggin
—OUCH!—

and Grandma tried to soothe her with a kiss.

"I will kiss it, make it better."
Grandma leaned to take a peek.

"NO KISSIES!"

Rissy chirruped with a most emphatic squeak.

"You should teach that girl some manners,"
Grandma Lovebird briskly cooed.
"We know lovebirds all love kisses.
I think Rissy's being rude."

In the mornings, Rissy rushed to class to claim her favorite spot
on the rug between two friendly chicks, who smiled and sang a lot.

Every day they scooted nearer;

they grew closer every week,

till **"NO KISSIES!"**

Rissy chirruped with a most emphatic squeak.

Rissy's new friends felt rejected,
flapped and fussed and made a scene.

"We know lovebirds all love kisses.
We think Rissy's being mean."

"Am I mean, Mom?" Rissy wondered,
"or confused or rude or sick?

"Are you certain I'm a lovebird?
Are you sure that I'm your chick?

"Kissies make my tummy icky.
I feel worried, weird, and wrong.

"If I can't show love with kissies,
then I'll never quite belong."

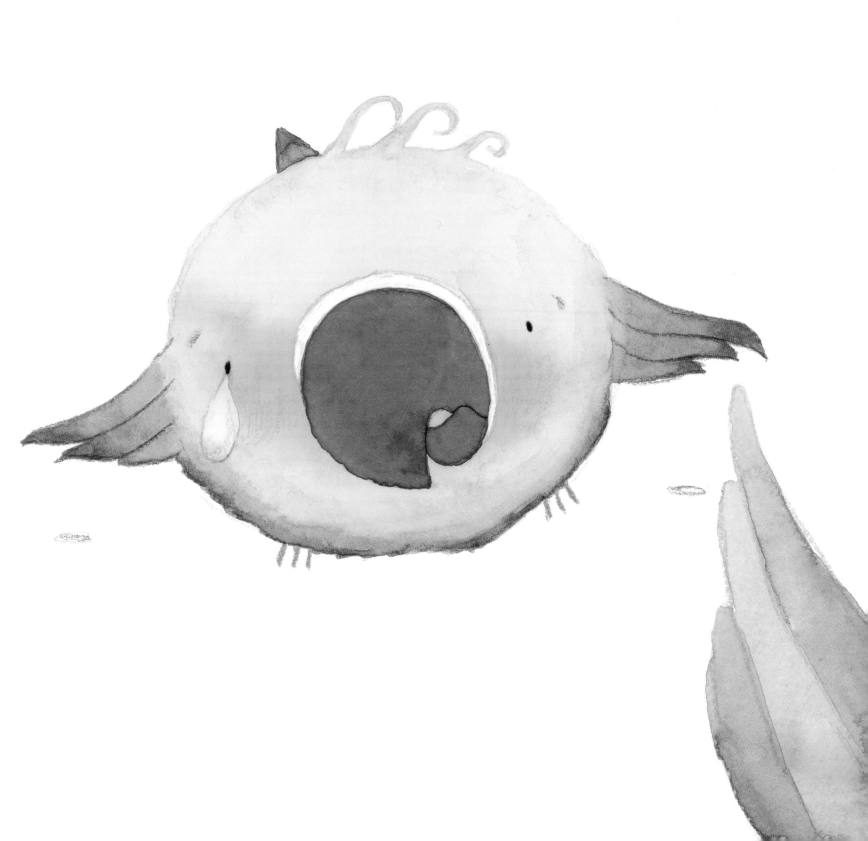

"Oh, my Rissy," said her mother,
"there is NOTHING wrong with you.

"While it's true you don't like kisses,
you're a lovebird through and through.

"Your body and your heart are yours,
and **you** choose how to share.

"You get to pick the ways
you want to show us that you care."

Reassured now, Rissy spoke up,
for she had some things to say.

"Yes, I love you all," she chirruped,
"But I'll show it my own way.

"Some birds share their love with kissies,
but they're not my favorite things.

"I like singing songs together,
sitting close, and holding wings.

"I see love in cards and cookies,
flying flips, and sky-high hugs.

"With no kissies to upset me,
I feel safe and warm and snug."

From then on, when Rissy played with friends
or when she bumped her head,
when her heart was feeling oh so full
or when she went to bed,
she gave feather fives and nuzzles,
she shared snuggles cheek to cheek.

"I'M A LOVEBIRD,"

Rissy chirruped with a most emphatic squeak.

A Note to Kids

We all like different things.

Different foods. Different music. Different ways to show we care.

So how do you know what someone else likes? You ask!

We can all be kind and respectful by asking before we touch.

We ask, "Can I give you a hug?" We ask, "Do you want to hold my hand?"

We ask, "How do you like to show that you care?"

We can all use our voices to say "no" to things we don't like.

Your body is your own, and no one else's. You decide what you like and don't like. It is your choice how to touch and be touched.

You don't have to get or give any touches that you don't want.

Use your voice. Say, "No." Say, "I don't like that."

We can all feel safe and special by listening and respecting choices.

When you say *no*, people should listen to your voice and respect your choice.

When friends say *no*, you should listen to their voices and respect their choices.

If someone touches you in ways you do not like, say *no*. Tell a trusted adult.

You know each person likes different things. You know each person's body is their own.

Listening to voices and respecting choices shows that you care about others.

Using your voice shows that you care about yourself too!

A Note to Caregivers

Bodily autonomy: your body is yours alone—and you are the one who gets to decide how to touch and be touched

Consent: permission—that people should ask permission to touch you, and you should ask permission to touch them

A boundary: a limit—something a person is comfortable or not comfortable with

Sensory processing: the way our brains interpret the information that comes from our senses

It is never too early to teach children about bodily autonomy, consent, and boundaries. These concepts are as important for toddlers as they are for teens. Teaching and modeling them will help the young children in your care grow up respecting their own bodies, their own feelings, and the bodies and feelings of others.

So how do you know what kinds of touches someone else prefers? It's simple. You ask, and you respect the answer. Talking about and practicing "ask and respect" is key to teaching children about bodily autonomy and consent.

Additionally, children with sensory processing issues may have challenges organizing and interpreting sensory information. They may be overstimulated or understimulated by certain sights, sounds, smells, textures, touches, or tastes. Some people with sensory processing issues can have negative reactions to hugs, kisses, or other touches common with affection—but they still want and need to show and be shown affection. Practicing "ask and respect" helps young children with sensory processing issues learn to communicate touches they like and to feel safe, respected, and loved.

Key Practices
- Never force a child to hug, kiss, or touch someone.
- Always ask a child before touching them.
- Teach that *no* and *stop* are key words. Stop as soon as someone says them.
- Model offering alternatives. "Do you want a hug or a high five?"
- When certain touches are necessary (holding hands to cross the street, getting a shot), offer the child ways to exert control of the situation.
- Teach children to identify and speak to a trusted adult if someone touches them in a way they do not like.

For more information on bodily autonomy and consent, visit https://www.safesecurekids.org.
For more information on sensory processing issues, visit https://www.understood.org.

For my Marissa, who is often emphatic —K.H.

Carolrhoda Books®
An imprint of Lerner Publishing Group, Inc.
241 First Avenue North
Minneapolis, MN 55401 USA

For reading levels and more information, look up this title at www.lernerbooks.com.

Designed by Emily Harris.
Main body text set in Mikado Regular.
Typeface provided by HVD Fonts.
The illustrations in this book were created with watercolor.

Library of Congress Cataloging-in-Publication Data

Names: Howes, Katey, author. | Engle, Jess, 1983- illustrator.
Title: Rissy no kissies / Katey Howes ; illustrated by Jess Engle.
Description: Minneapolis : Carolrhoda Books, [2021] | Audience: Ages 4–9. | Audience: Grades 2–3. | Summary: "A lovebird who doesn't like kisses? Rissy's friends and family wonder if she's sick, confused, or rude. But kisses make Rissy uncomfortable. Can she show everyone there's not one right way to share affection?" —Provided by publisher.
Identifiers: LCCN 2020022276 (print) | LCCN 2020022277 (ebook) | ISBN 9781541597983 (trade hardcover) | ISBN 9781728417394 (ebook)
Subjects: CYAC: Stories in rhyme. | Kissing—Fiction. | Individuality—Fiction. | Lovebirds—Fiction.
Classification: LCC PZ8.3.H8417 Ris 2021 (print) | LCC PZ8.3.H8417 (ebook) | DDC [E]—dc23

LC record available at https://lccn.loc.gov/2020022276
LC ebook record available at https://lccn.loc.gov/2020022277

Manufactured in the United States of America
3-51119-48668-6/10/2021